This book belongs to

_____

THE NIGHT BEFORE CHRISTMAS

by Clement Clarke Moore

Illustrated by Ruth Sanderson

Little, Brown and Company

Boston   New York   Toronto   London

First Edition

Library of Congress Cataloging-in-Publication Data

Moore, Clement Clarke, 1779–1863.
   The night before Christmas / by Clement Clarke Moore ; illustrated by Ruth Sanderson. — 1st ed.
       p.   cm.
   Summary: Presents the well-known poem about an important Christmas visitor.
   ISBN 0-316-57963-7
   1. Santa Claus — Juvenile poetry. 2. Christmas — Juvenile poetry.
3. Children's poetry, American. [1. Santa Claus — Poetry.
2. Christmas — Poetry. 3. American poetry. 4. Narrative poetry.]
I. Sanderson, Ruth, ill. II. Title.
PS2429.M5N5   1997
811'.2 — dc20   96-28153

10 9 8 7 6 5 4 3 2

NIL

Published simultaneously in Canada by Little, Brown & Company (Canada) Limited

Printed in Italy

The paintings for this book were done in Winsor & Newton oils
on Giverny canvas.

For Eric and Diane

'TWAS THE NIGHT BEFORE CHRISTMAS,

When all through the house

Not a creature was stirring, not even a mouse;

The stockings were hung by the chimney with care,

In the hopes that Saint Nicholas soon would be there;

The children were nestled all snug in their beds,

While visions of sugarplums danced in their heads;

And Mama in her kerchief and I in my cap

Had just settled down for a long winter's nap,

When out on the lawn there arose such a clatter,

I sprang from my bed to see what was the matter.

Away to the window I flew like a flash,

Tore open the shutters and threw up the sash.

The moon on the breast of the new-fallen snow

Gave the lustre of midday to objects below,

When, what to my wondering eyes should appear,

But a miniature sleigh and eight tiny reindeer,

With a little old driver, so lively and quick,

I knew in a moment it must be Saint Nick.

More rapid than eagles his coursers they came,

And he whistled and shouted and called them by name:

"Now, Dasher! Now, Dancer! Now, Prancer and Vixen!

On, Comet! On, Cupid! On, Donder and Blitzen!

To the top of the porch! To the top of the wall!

Now dash away! Dash away! Dash away all!"

As dry leaves that before the wild hurricane fly,

When they meet with an obstacle, mount to the sky;

So up to the housetop the coursers they flew,

With the sleigh full of toys, and Saint Nicholas, too.

And then, in a twinkling, I heard on the roof

The prancing and pawing of each little hoof.

As I drew in my head, and was turning around,

Down the chimney Saint Nicholas came with a bound.

He was dressed all in fur, from his head to his foot,

And his clothes were all tarnished with ashes and soot;

A bundle of toys he had slung on his back,

And he looked like a peddler just opening his pack.

His eyes — how they twinkled! His dimples, how merry!

His cheeks were like roses, his nose like a cherry!

His droll little mouth was drawn up like a bow,

And the beard on his chin was as white as the snow;

He had a broad face and a little round belly,

That shook when he laughed, like a bowlful of jelly.

He was chubby and plump, a right jolly old elf,

And I laughed when I saw him, in spite of myself;

A wink of his eye and a twist of his head

Soon gave me to know I had nothing to dread.

He spoke not a word but went straight to his work,

And filled all the stockings; then turned with a jerk,

And laying a finger aside of his nose,

And giving a nod, up the chimney he rose;

He sprang to his sleigh, to his team gave a whistle,

And away they all flew like the down of a thistle.

But I heard him exclaim, ere he drove out of sight,

"Happy Christmas to all, and to all a good night!"